THERE WAS ONCE A GROUP OF TREES
who were fed up with living in a deep, dark,
and crowded valley. So they decided
to move to the top of a nearby hill.

Here, they could enjoy the sun on their
leaves, fresh air through their branches, and
the best view for miles around.

But trees cannot walk without magic.
And the creatures that followed them created
an enchanted forest. Outside, *darker*
creatures wanted the magic for themselves.

This is the story of how a little boy came
into the forest, but left the way open...

For Gina, Mark, Matthew and Nicholas
Thank you to Anne McNeil and David Mackintosh

Love to Monika

First edition for the United States, its territories and
dependencies, the Philippine Republic, and Canada
published in 2003 by Barron's Educational Series, Inc.

Copyright © David Melling 2003

The right of David Melling to be identified as the
author and illustrator of this Work has been asserted
by him in accordance with the Copyright, Designs and
Patents Act 1988.

First published in the United Kingdom in 2003 by
Hodder Children's Books, a division of Hodder Headline
Limited, 338 Euston Road, London NW1 3BH

All inquiries should be addressed to:
Barron's Educational Series, Inc.
250 Wireless Boulevard
Hauppauge, New York 11788
http://www.barronseduc.com

Library of Congress Catalog Card No. 2002117175
International Standard Book No. 0-7641-5675-6

Printed in Hong Kong
9 8 7 6 5 4 3 2 1

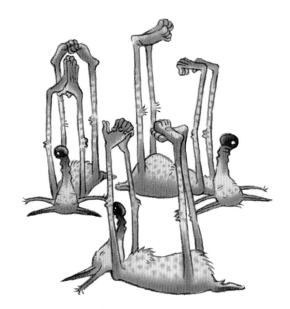

THE TALE OF
JACK FROST

BARRON'S

It was a crisp and frosty morning.
Woodwind and Woffle were out collecting
snow-beetles when they found a boy.

A *real* boy, asleep in the snow.

They hopped around in circles.
"What to do! What to do!" they squeaked.

Shadows came bobbing and gliding toward them from every direction.

Jack was so happy he tingled all over. He could feel himself
getting lighter and lighter. Then he was flying.

Woodwind and Woffle rushed to meet Jack.

"No more goblins! No more goblins!" they sang.

"We must celebrate at once," said the unicorn, who
could see how brave Jack had been.
Everyone cheered with delight.

All night there was music, magic,
and worm-juice surprise.

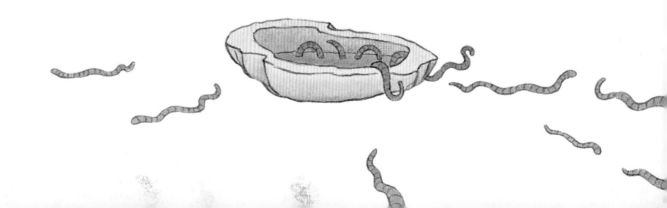

Jack had been making magic ice puddles with snail glue,
when he heard angry slippy noises:

SQUEEE-DUNK!!!

As soon as the goblins touched the ice puddles they froze.
Within moments there were frozen goblins everywhere.

Jack skipped to the ice statues and gave them a frosty
sunflower. "Here you are," he laughed. "This is your sun.
These sunflowers will warm you up and set you free.
This is the only magic you will see tonight!"

The goblins could only stare with stiff grins and
chattering teeth.

But, by the time they reached the stone tower, the ice had melted and the sun had gone. All they had were wet hands.

"We've been tricked," growled King Gobbledegook.

With screams of rage, they raced back to Jack.

Well, the goblins were delighted. They lifted the "frozen sun" and ran off.
They didn't even say thank you.

"No!" said Jack, and pointed at the reflection of the moon. "Look, *there* is the sun." He dipped his finger into the lake. With wide eyes the goblins gawped as a thin film of frost crept and crackled and glistened across the lake.

In moments it had turned to ice.

The goblins followed Jack to the lake. They were very excited.
"First, you must make a circle around the lake," said Jack. "Now look into the lake and tell me what you see."

The goblins stared. Nothing. Then a small goblin, who had medals for thinking, sprang to his feet. "Water!" he shouted.

"Oh yes," they said, giggling and nudging
each other in the ribs, "we promise."

Jack knew they were lying, but he had an idea.

"That's easy!" said Jack. "Every night the sun goes to sleep in a lake by the forest. It is full of magic and easy to catch."

"Ooooooo!" said the goblins. They were impressed.

"But if I show you how to catch the sun you must promise never to go into the enchanted forest," said Jack.

King Gobbledegook plucked Jack from the sack.
He was surrounded by cabbage-smelling goblins.
"Hello," said Jack, bravely, and touched the royal
dimply nose.

"Eeeeeaaarrrgghh!" squealed the king,
"he's freezing!"

"WE WANT THE MAGIC!!" roared the goblins.

"I'LL do the shouting," snapped King Gobbledegook.
He turned to Jack. "YOU'RE going to tell us how to
get this magic," he said, "or there'll be trouble.
And YOU'LL be in it."

The other goblins sniggered.

That night, Jack Frost was playing with a friendly pack of Bing Bong Bandylegs. These were large animals, but they scared easily. Indeed, at the first sign of danger they would roll onto their backs and pretend to be asleep.

So when a goblin stumbled across Jack Frost, with a bunch of snoring creatures, he stuffed him into a sack and scurried off, back to the goblins' lair.

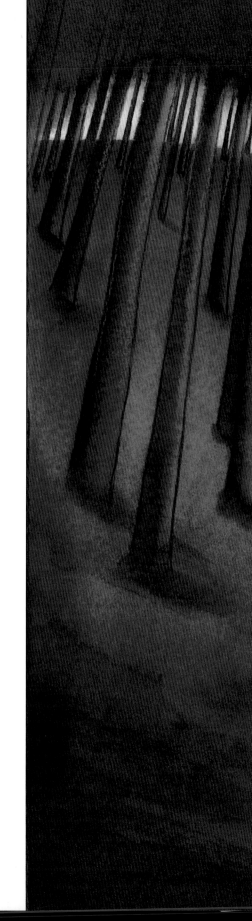

Now, in the dank valley with its curling mist there lived many thick stubby creatures with green oily skin.

Goblins!!

They smelled of boiled cabbage and liked to make rude noises just for fun. Clever, they were not. When they heard that Jack Frost, a *real* boy, had been shown the magic of the enchanted forest they were furious. Goblins believed that the magic should be theirs.

Now the forest was open – this was their chance.

But his skin was snow white and always ice cold.
Whatever he touched for more than a few
moments turned to frost.

And so the creatures named him Jack Frost.
Only the unicorn remained nervous.
"Something bad will happen," he snorted.

And before long, it did...

They all taught the boy
what they knew.

He mixed rare potions and
unusual soups – his favorite
was worm-juice surprise.

He was quick to understand magic,
and he was *very* good with snail glue.

But Woodwind and Woffle were
hopping again.
"Too cold! Too cold!" they cried.
"He needs our help."
Cowslip agreed. He prepared an
ointment and bathed the boy's eyes.

Slowly, the boy awoke.

They asked him many questions,
but he remembered nothing.
Not even his name.

Cowslip, a tall and gentle creature
with hairy knees, spoke first.
"What shall we do with him?"
he asked.

The unicorn stepped forward.

"We are in danger," he said.
"Where he came in, others will
follow."

Unicorns and woodhoppers and beezels appeared.
Owls and magpies and skitlets dropped from bending
branches. Funny looking creatures peered around each
other, and even the trees shuffled forward for a better look.

Jack never did remember his past, but, at last, he knew where he belonged. And the goblins? Well, they're still looking for the magic, and they're still grumpy. But that's goblins for you.

Sometimes on cold winter nights you may see
swirling shapes of ice on your windows,
or frosty ice puddles in your garden.

Yes! Jack Frost likes to visit places outside the enchanted forest
and he always leaves little spells of magic —
to protect you from the smell of boiled cabbage.